5-MINUTE STORIES MINECRAFTERS

EXTREME STORIES FROM THE EXTREME HILLS

Also by Greyson Mann:

Five-Minute Minecrafter Mysteries

The Creeper Code

Secrets of an Overworld Survivor

Lost in the Jungle

When Lava Strikes

Wolves vs. Zombies

Never Say Nether

The Creeper Diaries

Mob School Survivor

Creeper's Got Talent

THE SPIDER'S BITE

"I found a cave!"

Anthony's voice rang off the jagged cliffs and stone spires of the Extreme Hills.

Sophia sprinted toward the sound, trying not to slide in the rocks. She heard Zack bounding down the hill behind her. Then he raced by, his hulking body blocking her view of the rushing river below.

"Wait for me!" she cried, but her pack was heavy. *Slosh, slosh, slosh* . . .

Zack turned and grinned. "You sound like a wet, sloppy slime!"

"It's . . . the milk," said Sophia, trying to catch her breath. "You'll . . . thank me for it . . . later!"

Zack shook his blonde head. "Not a chance!" Then he turned on the speed, leaving her in his dust.

Zack had been disappointed when Sophia came back from a field of cows with nothing but milk. *But I don't kill peaceful mobs,* she reminded herself. *I'm saving my sword for whatever we find in that cave!*

Anthony looked tiny standing at the mouth of it. For a moment, Sophia feared the cave might swallow him right up. But his brown eyes gleamed with excitement. "Do you think we'll find a treasure chest? Or even emeralds?" He rubbed his hands together.

"Maybe," said Zack, pushing past him. "But I *know* we'll find some mobs to fight." He pulled his sword from his sheath and took the lead.

The first thing they found were rusty minecart tracks. Sophia squinted into the darkness, trying to see where they went. "There must be an abandoned mineshaft not far from here."

"Here's the cart!" Zack called from up ahead.

The minecart looked sturdy, but Sophia wasn't ready to climb in. Anthony must have felt the same way, because his voice cracked when he asked, "Where do you think it'll take us?"

"Straight to your treasure chest," said Zack. "C'mon! Let's go!"

When Anthony climbed in, Sophia followed. "Here goes nothing," she said to herself as Zack pulled the long wooden lever and hopped in behind her.

Soon they were coasting down a rickety track, deep into the black tunnel. As Sophia's eyes adjusted to the dark, she made out the wooden beams of the mineshaft. The cart sped by cobblestone walls, close enough to touch—if she dared reach out her hand.

A dip in the track sent them soaring straight down. Sophia's stomach lurched. She tightened her grip on the sides of the cart.

They veered left, then right, and then left again. Anthony toppled sideways into her lap. "Sorry!" His voice sounded strained.

Then the cart climbed slowly upward. Was there something on the tracks ahead? Miners carrying torches? Sophia leaned forward to see.

Two glowing red eyes stared back at her.

"Spider! Cave spider!"

Her words were muffled by the *click-clack* of the cart as it rolled downward

again and veered right, narrowly missing the red-eyed mob.

Then they came to a sudden, screeching halt.

Sophia could barely breathe. "Everyone okay?" she whispered.

Zack kicked into action behind her. "We need torches!" His voice rang off the walls of the mineshaft.

As Sophia fumbled in her pack for her torch, Zack's lit up, casting a warm glow on the cobblestone. Now they could see the narrow hallway.

"C'mon!" Zack was already racing down it. "I see another room!"

Anthony sprang forward, too, as if he could already see his precious treasure chest. But Sophia's legs felt wobbly beneath her.

As Zack and Anthony disappeared around a corner, she took stock of the mineshaft. Why were there no torches? How long had it been since someone had mined here?

She raised her torch and glanced up. That's when she saw them.

Cobwebs—thick, white, and sticky. And that could mean only one thing.

"Spiders!" she cried, sprinting toward her friends.

Too late.

Zack was surrounded by a ring of squealing cave spiders. He struck the black beasts with his sword, swinging wildly from side to side.

When Sophia saw the fire-filled spawner in the middle of the room, she sucked in her breath. If the spawner kept spitting out spiders, she and her friends would never make it. She had to destroy it!

She stepped toward the spawner, reaching for her pickaxe.

"Sophia! Help!"

Anthony's panicky voice stopped her in her tracks. She spun around.

She could barely see her friend dangling from the back wall, just above a treasure chest. He was bound by a cocoon of sticky spider webs. As a hungry, red-eyed mob scuttled slowly toward Anthony, Sophia screamed.

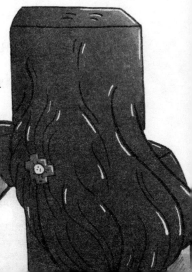

"No!"

She raced forward and struck the spider with her pickaxe—hard. The mob glowed red hot with anger. It whirled around to lunge at her. This time, she came back with her sword. She struck with everything she had, backing the spider up against a wall.

Finally it fell.

But another one would take its place if she didn't free Anthony. *Now.*

She slashed with her sword at the web that bound him. He struggled to free his arms and legs. Finally he broke away and landed with a *thud* on the chest below.

"Are you okay?" she asked.

He nodded. But as he stared at something over her shoulder, his eyes widened. "Zack!"

Sophia turned, too.

Whack, whack, whack . . . Zack was striking the spawner with his pickaxe, but with his final blow, a spider struck *him*.

The spider's venom hit him hard and fast. As he slumped to the ground, Sophia grabbed her sack and rushed to his side.

"Sit up," she ordered.

His eyes rolled backward, but he lifted his head just enough for her to raise the bottle of milk to his lips.

"Drink."

Most of the milk dribbled down his chin, but he must have swallowed enough. Slowly the color came back to his cheeks and he opened his eyes wide. "What happened?"

"Cave spiders, that's what. You destroyed the spawner, but the spiders nearly destroyed *you*. So, you're welcome."

"For what?"

"For the milk. I told you it would come in handy."

Zack smiled, just barely.

But Anthony wasn't smiling as he lifted the lid of the treasure chest. "We're too late," he said, his shoulders slumping. "It's empty. Someone must have gotten here first."

Sophia shrugged. "So let's collect a different kind of treasure." She pulled out her shears and started snipping at a cobweb. "You never know when string might come in handy."

She was surprised when Zack stepped up beside her to help. *This* time, he must have believed her.

LAVA STRIKES

Clink!

As Anthony tapped the wall once more with his pickaxe, a chunk of stone fell to the ground. Something sparkled from deep within the wall.

No way.

He could barely say the word out loud. "Diamonds?"

Another careful tap with the pickaxe revealed more bluish-white flecks. "Diamonds!" he hollered to his friends.

He'd struck it rich! Not by finding an overflowing treasure chest, but these were diamonds all the same. He would just have to work a little harder to set them free.

Clink, clink, clink!

"Anthony!" Sophia called from behind.

"Not now," he said. "I've almost got this big one loose!"

"Anthony!" This time it was Zack calling his name.

"Just a second!"

Zack hollered something else
that Anthony couldn't hear over the
rushing water.

Wait, water? He didn't remember
passing a pool or stream on his way
into this cave. So where was the sound
coming from?

He pressed his ear to the wall and
heard it louder: a bubbling, rushing
sound. As his cheek brushed against
the stone, he felt the heat—and
quickly pulled away.

Lava!

Anthony knew he had to run, but
he couldn't. He couldn't even *move*.

The stone wall gave way as if in
slow motion. That orange, angry river

of lava streamed out, first through cracks and then through gaping holes. Anthony tripped backward, trying to escape. Then he struck something hard from behind. The back wall of the cave. He was trapped!

Someone or something yanked his arms, pulling him up onto a rocky ledge. As lava licked at his feet, he stared at the flames, suddenly realizing they were coming from his own pantleg. His clothes were on fire!

"Get down! Roll!" Sophia ordered. She was here too, high on the rocky ledge.

Then Anthony felt Zack's strong arms knock him to the ground and push him, until he was rolling across the cool rock.

Smoke billowed from his pants, but the fire was out.

"The lava's rising," Sophia cried. "We have to climb higher!"

Anthony wasn't sure his legs would work. But when Zack pulled him to his feet, he ran—*fast* behind his friends. Until they hit another wall.

"There's nowhere to go!" Sophia's face glowed pale white against the dark stone wall.

"Except up," said Zack, pointing. "Another ledge. Let's go."

Anthony stepped onto Zack's back to reach the sharp rim of rock. Would he have the strength to pull himself up?

His feet scrabbled at the wall, trying to find traction. He scrunched his eyes shut and slowly heaved himself upward, groaning, until his body sprawled sideways on the ledge.

He scooted backward to make room for Sophia and then Zack, who had

somehow found a foothold on the smooth wall below.

Sweat poured from Anthony's forehead as he stared down at the ocean of lava. It was still rising. "Are we high enough?" he asked.

Sophia shrugged. "I hope so. But we should keep moving, just in case."

"Move *where*?" Anthony wasn't sure he wanted to know.

Sophia pointed to a thin strip of rock that crossed the cavern. The makeshift bridge led to a wider room on the other side. "I see light," she said. "That's our way out."

"She's right," said Zack. "Let's go." He crossed the bridge first, putting one foot in front of the other as if he were on a tightrope.

Sophia took her time, dropping to her knees as she neared the end.

Then Anthony was alone, with just a crumbly stone tightrope separating him from his friends—and from a fiery fall to his death in the lava pit below.

He swallowed hard and took his first step, wishing there were something—anything!—to hold on to.

As he took another step, he wobbled.

"Don't look down!" Sophia cried.

He didn't. As his heart pounded in his chest, he stared somewhere between the stone bridge and Sophia's encouraging face.

Step by step, he inched his way across the stone, holding his arms out for balance.

When a wave of cool air greeted him, he knew he'd made it. That's when he collapsed into a heap on the solid ground.

Anthony couldn't speak for a minute or two. He shuddered, thinking about how close he had come to falling to his death. A wave of relief washed over him, followed by disappointment. He'd found his diamonds, and then lost them.

After another moment, his disappointment gave way to curiosity. "What were you guys trying to tell me back there in the diamond cave?" he asked, sitting up.

Sophia chuckled. "Lava," she said. "We were trying to tell you about the lava."

"Oh." He played with the singed hem of his pantleg. "I guess I was too busy worrying about the diamonds. And I didn't even get any—not a single one."

"Wrong," said Zack. "You got one." He pulled a stone-encrusted diamond from his pocket. "You had this in your hand when we pulled you up onto the ledge." He smiled and handed it over.

Anthony cupped his fingers around the sparkly stone, feeling its sharp edges. *Ouch!*

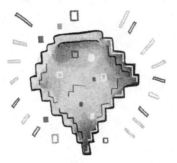

But they reminded him that where there are treasures, there might also be danger. And he wouldn't forget again.

TRAPPED!

Something wasn't right. The hairs stood up on Zack's arms as he stepped into the dark mineshaft. *Go slow*, said the voice in his head. *Proceed with caution.*

"What's the holdup?" whispered Sophia from behind. "Is there a mob?"

Zack shook his head. "Just a . . . feeling," he said.

"A what?" called Anthony, who was bringing up the rear. "Let me see!" He pushed forward, accidentally knocking Sophia into Zack.

That's when Zack felt the ground give way beneath him. "Woahhhhhh!"

He fell into darkness and landed with a sloppy *smack* on something wet and squishy.

Smuck! Smack!

"Ouch!"

"Ow!"

His friends landed beside him. At least he *hoped* it was them.

"Are you guys okay?" he whispered, wiggling his own fingers and toes to be sure he wasn't hurt.

"Yeah," came Sophia's muffled voice. "But what's that *smell*?"

Zack patted the sticky ground beneath him. He lowered his nose to take a whiff, and then quickly sat back up. "Ugh. I think we just landed in a zombie trap."

Anthony whimpered.

"Wait, you mean we're sitting in . . . *rotten flesh*?" Sophia gagged.

"Don't worry about the smell," said Zack, jumping up. His feet slid sideways in the slippery meat. "Worry about the zombies. Do you hear any?" He took a slow spin in the darkness.

"Somebody light a torch!" cried Anthony.

"I would, but I can't find my pack!" Sophia's voice sounded far away.

"I dropped mine, too," said Zack. "But let's stay calm. There must be a door here somewhere. The miner who built this needs to come down to collect mob drops."

Sophia snorted. "Judging by the smell and the piles of meat on the floor, that miner hasn't come down here in a very long time."

"So no one is coming for us?" asked Anthony, his voice rising. "How are we going to get out?"

"Just look for a door," said Zack. He waved his arm in the darkness, searching for a wall. Instead, his fingers brushed against something furry.

He heard a soft squeal, and two glowing eyes pierced the darkness just inches from his face.

"Spider!" he cried as he jumped backward. He fumbled in the dark for his sword.

"Where?" Sophia's voice bounced off the walls.

"Here!" shouted Zack. But when he swung with his sword, he struck nothing but stone. His arms tingled with the impact. As he tried to pull the sword back out, he grunted. It wouldn't budge. "Great. Now my sword's stuck!"

"I've got mine!" cried Sophia. "Where's the spider?"

"I don't know!"

Zack froze, listening for the telltale squeal or scuttle of legs across the flesh-covered floor.

He heard nothing, except a scraping sound.

"What's that?" Sophia squeaked.

Zack's mouth went dry. "I don't know."

There it was again. *Scritch, scritch, scritch . . .*

Zack whirled around, prepared to fight whatever mob they were facing.

Then a spark lit the room—and Anthony's face. He smiled. "Flint and steel," he said. "I dropped my torch, but I always carry flint and steel in my pack."

As he lit a small piece of wool, light danced across the stone walls.

"There's the door!" cried Zack, pointing.

"And there's your spider!" said Anthony, chuckling.

"Where?" Zack followed Anthony's pointed finger toward the tiny black mob dangling from a corner. It wasn't a spider at all. It was a *bat*.

"Oh, he's cute!" said Sophia. "Hey, little buddy!"

Zack wanted to laugh, too. But everything in him told him to *run*. Spiders, he could handle. But bats gave him the willies! How do you fight something so small? Something with fangs? Something with wings?

He yanked on his sword, freeing it from the wall. And then he ran toward the door.

"Zack, wait!"

But he didn't. He burst through the door, raced up the mossy stone steps, and didn't stop until he was standing in a hallway safely lit with glowing torches.

"Zack, what's wrong?" Sophia was by his side seconds later.

"Bats," he muttered. "I don't do bats."

Her face broke into a smile. "Let me get this straight. You don't mind sitting in a pile of zombie flesh. You'll battle cave spiders till their death. But a tiny, harmless, cute little bat freaks you out?"

"Yup," said Zack, sinking down to sit on the floor. "Secret's out."

"What secret?" asked Anthony. He slowed to a stop next to them, and then leaned over to catch his breath.

Sophia smiled. "Nothing," she said. "Zack here was just saying we should move on before any mobs strike." She helped him up.

Zack mouthed a "thank you" to Sophia.

Then he took one last glance upward, slid his sword back into its sheath, and hurried after his friends.

DEATH BY STARVATION

"I'm starving," groaned Anthony. "Don't we have any food left?"

Sophia nodded. "Sure! Apples, fish, bread, mushroom stew. But it's not time to eat yet. Don't you remember the rules of exploring the Overworld? Make your food last."

"She's probably right," Zack chimed in. "The longer our food lasts, the better chance you've got of finding that treasure chest."

Anthony sighed. "Yeah, okay. But I'm so hungry, I swear I could eat rotten flesh."

"Gross." Sophia wrinkled her nose. "Let's hope we never have to do that." She slung the navy-blue sack of food over her shoulder so that Anthony wouldn't be tempted to break into it. Then she followed Zack through the deep ravine.

A gentle breeze tickled her hair as she turned her face upward. A thin sliver of sky shone through a crack in the cavern, and water dripped down the walls into a cave pool nearby.

"Hey, is this Redstone?" Zack called.

Sophia hurried to catch up. Sure enough, Zack stood in front of a stone wall speckled with Redstone ore. "Let's mine some. Grab your pickaxe!"

She and Zack swapped their swords for axes and piled their belongings against the far wall. As they began clinking away at the stone, Anthony joined them. And soon, they had a pile of Redstone at their feet.

"*Now* can we eat?" Anthony whined.

"I vote yes!" said Zack.

Sophia raised her hands at her sides. "I guess I'm outnumbered." But the truth was, hunger nipped at her own stomach, too. She could taste that juicy apple already!

Then she heard it—the soft *hiss* that meant trouble was near.

When she whirled around, the creeper stood just a few feet away, *between* Sophia and the sack of food.

"What do we do?" she whispered to Zack. "Do you have your sword?"

"No! Everything is over there!"

Panic rose in Sophia's chest. By the time Zack

told her to run, her legs were already
moving. She raced down the hall
away from the creeper just as the mob
exploded. The sheer force lifted her
off her feet—and straight over the
slippery edge of a cave pool.

The icy-cold water took her breath
away. But as she sunk into the murky
pond, she realized she was safe. No
creeper could reach her here.

I wish I could say the same for our food, she thought sadly as she surfaced.

Zack had fallen into the pond, too. But where was Anthony?

She saw his outstretched body just a few feet away, covered with a thin layer of gunpowder.

"Anthony!" Sophia struggled to get out of the pond, but the mossy rock was too slippery.

Zack made it out first and was by Anthony's side in a second. "Hey, buddy. Wake up," he said, gently patting Anthony's face.

By the time Sophia got there, Anthony's eyes had fluttered open.

He's alive! she thought with relief. But he was too weak to hold up his head.

"He needs food," said Zack. "Pronto." He glanced down the hall, but the navy-blue sack had been blown to smithereens. When he turned back around, his worried eyes met Sophia's.

Guilt struck her like an iron sword. "It's gone," she said. "I know. I should have let him eat when he was hungry!"

Zack waved his hand. "Never mind that. Let's just find him something—fast."

But where? Sophia wondered. *We're in a deep ravine. We haven't seen a mineshaft in ages!*

"I'll go back up the mountain and look for meat," said Zack. "You stay with him. If I send you out there, you'll come back with pumpkins instead of pork." He gave her a small smile and then was gone.

As his footsteps faded, all Sophia could hear was Anthony's ragged breath and the *drip, drip, drip* of water running into the pond beside her.

"Anthony?" When she tapped his cheek, he opened his eyes. But they quickly closed again. "Anthony!"

Hot tears ran down Sophia's cheeks. *How can I help him?*

She jumped up and ran down the hall, hoping to find something—anything—left of their belongings.

The food sack was gone. Not even a charred hunk of fish remained. But beneath the rubble and gunpowder, she spotted the glint of an iron sword.

I have a weapon! Sophia told herself. *If I can kill a mob that drops food, I can help Anthony.*

But how could she lure mobs her way quickly?

Sophia glanced up at the torch lighting the hallway. It had been dark enough in here for a creeper to spawn, but she could make it even darker. She used her sword to strike down the torch. Then she sat in the darkness and waited.

When a low *moan* rose from the hallway, Sophia leaped to her feet. She'd never been so happy to hear a zombie!

"You might be eating rotten flesh after all," she said to Anthony, crouching low to give his shoulder a squeeze.

When she stood back up, the green, groaning mob staggered into view. And Sophia was ready.

It took just three strikes with the sword to bring that mob to the ground. Sophia attacked as if she were fighting for her life—no, *Anthony's* life. Then she searched for the zombie drop. Where was the rotten flesh?

Something orange caught her eye—a carrot. A crisp carrot! And next to that lay a golden potato.

"Oh, Anthony," she said, gathering the food quickly. "It's your lucky day!"

By the time Zack returned, she had managed to get Anthony to eat both vegetables. It wasn't enough to restore his health, but he was at least sitting upright.

"Did you get some meat?" she asked Zack.

Zack's cheeks flushed with embarrassment. "I forgot I didn't have my sword," he said. "So I had to go vegetarian—mushrooms and a few eggs from a chicken that I couldn't catch." He held up the food he had gathered in his cape.

Sophia laughed out loud. "It'll work," she said.

And it did.

Finally, Anthony started to look like Anthony again. When he said he was still hungry, Sophia handed Zack the sword she had used to kill the zombie.

"Zack will find you more food," she said to Anthony. "And this time, you can eat every last bite!"

DOWN IN THE DUNGEON

This is it, thought Anthony as he peered into the dimly lit room. *A dungeon. A real live dungeon!*

He looked past the monster spawner to the two treasure chests lining the cobblestone walls. A spark of excitement raced down his spine, like power along a trail of Redstone dust.

"Don't get too close to the spawner," Sophia cautioned. "We don't know which mobs it spawns yet."

But Zack blew right past her. "I'm on it," he said as he drew his sword.

"Zack!"

Too late. As the spawner came to life, the flame inside the cage swirled and spun. Then a newborn zombie was staggering toward them, as if he'd been in the room all along.

"Zombies! Ha!" cried Zack. "You guys head for the treasure. I'll handle these slowpokes."

Anthony dodged the zombie and tripped over the cobblestone toward a treasure chest. He could barely lift the

lid, his palms were so sweaty. What was inside? He couldn't wait to find out!

The first thing he saw was bread, which made his mouth water. But it was hardly a *treasure*.

He heard the *creak* of another lid and then saw Sophia digging in the other chest. "Ooh, an enchanted book!"

Now that's *a treasure,* thought Anthony, bummed that he hadn't found it in his own chest.

"Uff!" Zack took a hit in the battle behind them.

"Zack, be careful!" cried Sophia. "Just use your pickaxe and destroy the spawner!"

"Nah," said Zack, his voice cracking a bit. "It's more fun this way."

"You mean more *dangerous,*" said Sophia, sticking her head back into the chest.

The next thing Anthony struck was gold. "A gold ingot!" he cried.

"A golden apple!" cried Sophia at the exact same time.

"A gold what?" asked Zack.

"A gold ingot!" Anthony said again, turning to show Zack. "Hey, look out!"

The moment Zack took his eyes off the zombie, it attacked. And Zack went down hard.

"Zack!" Anthony dropped the ingot and reached for his sword. As he lunged at the zombie, he saw Sophia out of the corner of his eye. Was she coming to help? He hoped so. Zombie battles weren't his thing!

But Zack is in trouble, he reminded himself. So he did a slow dance around the zombie, striking and then retreating.

Thwack, thwack!

He heard Sophia attack, too—but not the zombie. She was striking the monster spawner with her pickaxe!

Stay focused, he told himself. *Keep your eyes on the zombie.*

He struck once more, and the green mob finally fell. A steaming hunk of rotten flesh plunked to the ground beside Zack.

At the same time, the spawner split in half.

And Zack sat up, rubbing his eyes. "What happened?"

"You got a little too confident!" Sophia scolded as she set down her pickaxe.

But Anthony felt a niggle of guilt. "Actually, I think I distracted him," he said. "With the gold, I mean."

He hurried back to the treasure chest and pulled out the gold ingot. Then he offered it to Zack. "Here, you should have it. You could craft a gold sword!"

Zack smiled. "Nah, you keep it. You're pretty good with a sword yourself!"

Sophia nodded. "You were really good, Anthony. Nice work!"

He shrugged, but the compliment found a home, spreading warmth throughout his chest.

"And you're pretty good with a pickaxe," Sophia said to Zack. "At least when you decide to *use* one to destroy a spawner instead of battling the zombies that came out." She cast a teasing glance his way.

Zack laughed. "Yeah, maybe next time, I'll take your advice and do just that."

ATTACK OF THE KILLER BAT

"Shh!" Sophia held her finger to her lips. "Is that lava I hear?"

Zack raised his ear to the wall. There was definitely *something* going on in the cave beyond. He heard scraping, squeaks, and scuttling. Was it silverfish?

He pulled out his sword and tiptoed toward the entrance.

As he stepped into the room, he looked down, examining every crack and crevice. Where were the bugs?

"Zack, look up!" Sophia cried.

As he raised his eyes to the ceiling, his stomach dropped. A sea of black bats flapped their wings and began swooshing around the cave. When a wing brushed against his face, Zack staggered backward.

He ran, not sure which way he was going—just *away* from the fluttering mob. His sword fell from his hand and *clanked* onto the ground. He tried to stop to grab it, but his feet tangled beneath him. And then he was doing somersaults.

He flipped once, twice, and then felt himself sliding . . . right off a rocky ledge.

His arms flailed at his sides, reaching for wood or rock or rope—anything!

Then he fell.

"Zack!" Sophia's worried face popped over the ledge above. "Are you okay?"

He rubbed his arm and sat up. "I think so."

"What happened?" she cried.

Then he remembered. "I *told* you I didn't like bats!" It sounded like an accusation, as if it were Sophia's fault that they'd just stepped into a bat family reunion. But he couldn't help it. Sometimes his fear had a funny way of turning into anger.

"Alright, I get it," said Sophia, holding her hands up. "But now we've gotta get you out of there. Stay put, and I'll go get some rope."

Zack studied his landing place. "Where am I going to go?" he joked quietly.

The torch that Sophia had left above cast fluttery shadows on the wall, bat-like shadows that made Zack's heart race. He squeezed his eyes shut and didn't open them again until he heard Sophia's voice.

"Grab this," she said. "Anthony and I wrapped it around a stone pillar. We'll pull. You just hang on."

He tried, but his left arm felt weak. So he tied the rope around his torso instead. As his friends pulled him up, inch by painful inch, he wished there were something he could do to help.

He grabbed a hold of the ledge as soon as he could. But as he pulled himself over the rim, he came face to face with . . . the *enemy*.

Zack screamed out loud.

And the tiny bat squealed back.

"Don't scare him!" cried Sophia, dropping the rope and hurrying toward the bat. "He's hurt!"

"Don't scare the killer bat?" whimpered Zack. "How about me?"

"Oh, you're alright." Sophia waved a hand. "He's more scared of you than you are of him."

"I doubt that," Zack whispered.

"Sophia found him on the ground," said Anthony, crouching beside the bat. "She thinks he broke his wing."

"Poor little thing," said Sophia. She reached out her hand, as if she wanted to *pet* the bat.

Zack swallowed hard. And forced himself to take a look.

The bat wasn't *quite* as scary close up. He was small and furry.

And if he didn't open his mouth, you'd never know he had fangs. He kept his wings folded around him, like a snug blanket.

Maybe he really is hurt, thought Zack. *Like me.* He pulled his own arm close.

Hisssss…

At first, Zack thought the sound was coming from the bat. Then he saw Sophia glance backward.

A creeper was coming. It was right behind them! But nobody moved.

Except the bat.

He wobbled into flight, sailing in a jagged line over Sophia's head. Toward the hissing creeper. And right into the explosion.

Ka-boooooom!!!

"No!" Sophia ran toward the sound instead of away from it. When she came back, tears cut a path 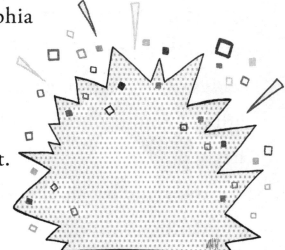 through the gunpowder on her face. "He's g-gone! He sacrificed himself to s-save us!"

"Who?" asked Zack.

"I think she means the bat," whispered Anthony.

"Oh." Zack was surprised to feel a twinge of sadness.

Then out of the darkness came a squeak. And the uneven flutter of wings. A bat flew in a wobbly arc around Sophia's head and landed on her shoulder.

"You came back!" she whispered, not daring to move.

"I told you he was a killer bat," said Zack softly. "But at least now we know he's the good kind."

"What kind is that?" asked Anthony.

Zack smiled. "The kind that kills *creepers.*"

THE ENDERMAN'S EVIL EYE

Anthony practically danced through the maze of stone corridors and down the spiral staircases. With every step, he kept his eyes open for treasure chests. In a stronghold like this, they could be anywhere!

Then he heard the sound that he had come to dread: hot, bubbling lava. "Where's it coming from?" he whispered.

"The End portal room," said Sophia. "We're almost there!"

Anthony held his breath as they stepped into the large chamber. In the middle of the room, a monster spawner rested atop a stone staircase. "What mob does it spawn?" he asked.

"Silverfish," said Zack. "Nasty, squealing little bugs. They're not nearly as much fun to kill as zombies."

"Good," said Sophia. "Then let's surround the spawner with torches and make sure it doesn't spawn *anything*."

She took the torch from her own pack and another from the wall. Then she placed the torches near the spawner. She tiptoed away, as if she might wake the silverfish.

Anthony took a slow, cautious walk around the room, steering clear of the two lava pools on either side of the entrance. As he passed the spawner and saw what was on the other side, he sucked in his breath. "Is that what I think it is?"

He pointed toward what could only be the End portal. A square of raised blocks framed a dark pit. And one of the blocks held something precious—a green Eye of Ender.

"Yup," said Zack. "Only eleven more Eyes of Ender, and we can journey to the End. Where's an Enderman when you need one?"

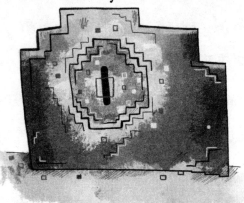

"Hey, don't joke about things like that," said Sophia.

Anthony started to laugh, and then froze. Because as soon as the words had left Sophia's mouth, something appeared in the hallway. Something tall, thin, and black. With long arms, like a spider standing upright.

As Anthony's eyes slid up the mob's torso, a voice in his head screamed at him. *Stop! Don't look it in the eye!*

"Enderman," he said under his breath, dropping his eyes to the floor. "Enderman! What do we do?"

"Don't look him in the eye," said Sophia. "Whatever you do, don't look him in the eye."

"Yeah, I know!" said Anthony, trying not to panic. "But what *should* I do?"

"Just play it cool," said Zack.

So Anthony did, studying his feet as if they were the most interesting things in the world. He played it cooler than cool—right up until the point when Sophia asked, "Is he carrying a treasure chest?"

Then his eyes flickered up, *just* for a second. But it was a second too long.

The Enderman stared back with glowing eyes.

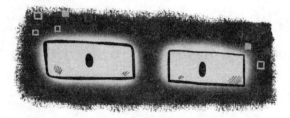

And when he saw Anthony looking up, those eyes narrowed. The Enderman shook with rage. He opened his mouth and released a menacing wail.

"He's coming!" cried Zack.

"Look out!" said Sophia. She ducked, as if the Enderman were a giant spider that might drop from the ceiling.

But Anthony stood perfectly still. What else could he do? Where could he go? He scrunched his eyes shut and braced for the attack.

It never came.

He heard the sounds of battle, as if they were coming from the room next door. *Thwack! Thwack!* Someone was fighting the Enderman. But who?

Anthony opened his eyes and dared to look up one more time.

Zack was striking the Enderman with his sword, hitting the mob in its long black legs. The Enderman wasn't carrying a treasure chest at all—it held a block of stone. And it *also* wasn't teleporting away. Why not?

Zack took another shot, and suddenly, the Enderman disappeared. "Where is it?" Zack shouted, spinning in a wild circle.

"Behind you!" cried Anthony, hoping he wasn't too late.

Zack spun, but the Enderman had already launched his attack. As Zack staggered backward, Anthony saw Sophia climbing the steps to the monster spawner. What was she doing?

She struck the torches away from the spawner with her sword. In the darkness that followed, the spawner came to life. The fiery ball at its center began spitting out silverfish.

One after another, the gray bugs scuttled down the steps.

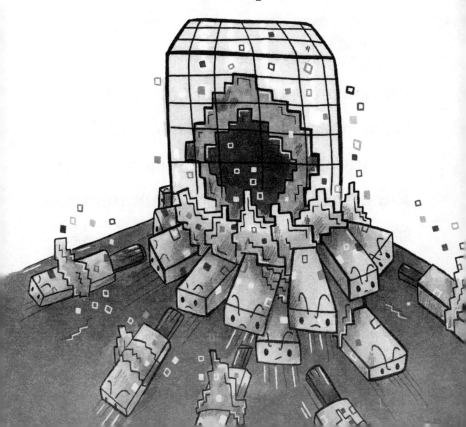

Sophia leaped out of the way, and the Enderman did too, teleporting to safer ground. But where?

Anthony tried to keep one eye on the silverfish and the other peeled for the Enderman. But as the bugs flowed toward him, he had to act fast.

"Help me with Zack!" cried Sophia. She was dragging him backward, toward the lava pit that bubbled between the monster spawner and the End portal.

Anthony dodged squealing silverfish and helped Sophia lug Zack onto the stone wall surrounding the lava. Zack settled onto the wall with a grunt, his head slumped forward.

Then Anthony hopped up, too. The silverfish swarmed the wall, climbing over one another as they tried to reach the top.

"We're safe up here," said Sophia. "As long as the Enderman doesn't come back." She pulled a golden apple out of her sack and held it up to Zack's mouth. "Take a bite, Zack. Just try."

"Where is the Enderman?" Anthony looked again—toward the entrance of the End portal room and past all of its shadowy corners.

Then his gaze bounced back to the last corner. And he found himself staring into a familiar pair of glowing eyes.

No! Anthony wanted to scream. *Not again!*

In the second he had to spare, he looked down at Zack, weak and pale. He had taken a bite of the golden apple, but it wouldn't cure him instantly. He wouldn't survive another Enderman battle—not now.

I have to get away from Zack, Anthony knew. *And take the teleporting Enderman with me.*

But silverfish swarmed the floor of the cavern. Where could he run? Onto the monster spawner? Into the pool of lava? In a split second, Anthony made his decision.

He leaped across the lava. As he
hit the stone wall on the other side,
he crouched low, wobbling to keep
his balance. And then the Enderman
appeared—not on the
wall, but *in* the lava pit!

The wailing, growling mob was there for just an instant before he teleported away.

"Woah," said Sophia. "That was amazing, Anthony!"

He tried to catch his breath. "Will he come back?"

"I don't think so," said Sophia. "He took damage from the lava. I think he's gone for good."

"I wish we could say the same about the silverfish," mumbled Zack, pulling his foot away from the teetering pile of squealing bugs below.

"Zack, you're back!" cried Anthony.

"And just in time, too," said Sophia. "We've got work to do."

She leaped from the wall to the stone steps of the monster spawner. Before another bug could scuttle out, she replaced the torches she had knocked down. As the flickering flames lit up the area around the spawner, the glowing orb at its center stopped spinning.

"How do we deal with the mobs that are already here?" asked Anthony.

"Lava," said Zack, pulling himself up to his feet. "We need to drown the silverfish in hot lava." He pulled out his pickaxe and hacked at the stone wall around the lava. When a block broke loose, the lava did, too.

As the hot, bubbling liquid spread across the floor, the silverfish squealed and scattered.

"But how do *we* get out?" cried Sophia.

"We run," said Zack, starting to sound like his old self again. He leaped onto the stone staircase that held the spawner and then jumped off, clearing the edge of the lava lake.

Anthony ran, too, following Zack across the room. He struck silverfish with his sword and dodged the widening rivers of lava.

When they finally reached the entrance to the End portal room, Zack paused to catch his breath. "Where's Sophia?"

"Here!" she called, pushing past them into the hallway. "Don't stop now. The lava is still spreading."

"Which way?" asked Zack. "Do you want to look for a treasure chest, Anthony? Strongholds are full of them."

Anthony flashed back to the memory of the Enderman carrying the stone block—the one that had *looked* like a treasure chest. Then he shook his head. "I've had enough of this stronghold's 'treasures' for one day. Let's get out of here."

"I'll second that," said Sophia. "Anthony, lead the way!"

AN UNDERWATER ESCAPE

Zack raised his torch to read the sign:
EMERALDS AHEAD.

"Do you think it's for real?" asked
Anthony.

"It *could* be," said Sophia. "Lots of
miners leave signs to mark their way
back to their mines."

"Or it could be a griefer messing
with us," Zack couldn't help pointing
out. When Anthony's face fell, he

added, "But we should check it out, just in case."

"This could be our last chance to mine some emerald ore," said Anthony.

"Exactly," said Sophia. "After all, who knows when we'll come back to the Extreme Hills again?"

"That settles it then," said Zack. "Let's go!"

The EMERALDS AHEAD sign pointed left down a long dark corridor. When the tunnel split in two, Zack waved his torch along the walls, hoping for another sign or message. "Which way?" he asked his friends. "It doesn't say!"

Anthony shrugged, but Sophia stared down the tunnel to the left, chewing her fingernail. "That way," she said. "Maybe."

So Zack turned left again. The tunnel opened up into a wide cavern, but Zack couldn't see any brilliant green emerald ore. He was inches away from the cave wall when something whizzed past his head.

Was it a bat? He brushed at his head with his hands and did a dance, hoping to avoid another bat encounter.

But as an arrow sped past his face and lodged itself in the wall, he suddenly knew just which mob he was facing.

"Skeletons!"
he shouted,
ducking down.

"They're on a ledge!"
cried Sophia. "We have to run
for cover!"

Before Zack could even get an
arrow into his own bow, skeleton
arrows began raining down all around.
He ran a zigzag path across the cavern,
pushing Anthony along ahead of him.

"In here!" said Sophia from up
ahead. "Quick!"

She led them into another tunnel
shooting off the cavern. Zack hid just
inside, slid an arrow into his bow, and
popped his head back into the cavern

to take a
shot.

"Yikes!"
This time,
the arrow
skimmed the
top of his head.
The skeleton that shot
it wasn't up on a ledge. He was right
behind them.

"Run!" shouted Zack.

As his friends barreled away down
the corridor, he tried to cover them,
running backward with his bow and
arrow drawn.

He got off a shot or two before finally
turning around and running, too.

The corridor narrowed—almost so tightly that Zack feared he couldn't get through. Then it opened up again. As he followed Sophia and Anthony into the cave at the end of the tunnel, he gasped.

"Emeralds!" cried Sophia. "Do you see them?"

"You bet I do," said Zack, taking it all in. "We found them."

"Thanks to the skeletons!" said Anthony. He had already drawn his pickaxe and was happily chipping away at the wall.

"Well, thanks to the skeletons, I also dropped my torch," said Sophia.

Zack studied the shadows in the corners of the cave. "Do you think something's going to spawn?"

Sophia shrugged, but he could read the worried expression on her face.

"Well, we'd better get mining then," he said. "Before something stands in our way."

He managed to collect a small pile of glittering green gems before he heard the first *hiss* of a creeper. "Where is it?" he asked.

"Here!" cried Anthony. He pointed toward the creeper that stood just a few feet away, blocking the entrance to the cave.

As Anthony dove, the creeper blew sky high.

BA-BOOM!!!

The noise was deafening. Zack clapped his hands over both ears, wishing the ringing would stop.

But he didn't cover his eyes. And he immediately saw the damage—and the danger.

The creeper had blown up the corridor that led into the cave. Crumbling rocks completely blocked the exit. And judging by the size of those boulders, it would take more than Zack and his two friends to roll them aside.

"Oh, no," breathed Sophia when she saw it, too. "Now what?"

"Now we look for another way out," said Zack, helping Anthony to his feet. "Look for cracks in the walls

or ceiling—and for blue sky above."
He tried to sound confident, but his
insides quivered like slime.

"Like that?" asked Anthony.

The crack along the ceiling was
paper-thin. Zack squinted, trying to
see out. He wished he had a ladder—
anything that would give him a better
view.

"If you follow the crack down, it
ends here," said Sophia, pointing
to a spot on the wall just above her.
"Maybe we can mine our way out!"

Zack shrugged. "I don't have any
better ideas," he admitted. "Let's do it."

With three pickaxes at work, the
rock gave way more quickly than

he'd expected. And as soon as it did, Zack was hit with another surprise—a torrent of water pouring into the cave.

"We must have come up under a pond!" cried Sophia. Her black hair was already drenched. "What do we do?"

Zack watched the water rise rapidly in the cave. If this was a pond, he knew it was fed by a river—and maybe one of the waterfalls that roared down through the Extreme Hills. The water wouldn't stop rising anytime soon.

He took a deep breath and faced his friends. "We swim."

With his pack strapped securely to his back, he took another deep breath and then forced himself through the hole, fighting the rushing water. *How deep is this pond?* he wondered. *Will I be able to swim to the top before running out of breath?*

He tried to stay calm as he took strong, sure strokes upward. When his head broke the surface of the water, he took in deep gulps of fresh air.

Then Sophia's dark head popped up beside him. She sputtered and sucked in air.

"Where's Anthony?" Zack cried. "Is he right behind you?"

Sophia nodded.

But the wait was painful. As Zack counted the seconds, he wondered,

Should I dive back down? Does Anthony need my help?

He counted to five and then took a deep breath. Just as he was preparing to dive, Anthony surfaced—finally!

"Are you okay?" asked Zack, swimming closer.

Anthony coughed and nodded. But he was using just one hand to tread water, which meant his head kept bobbing back under.

"What's wrong with your arm?" asked Zack.

Anthony grinned and showed both hands above the water. "Nothing. I was just using it to check the emeralds in my pocket. They're still there."

Zack threw back his head and laughed. Then he caught sight of the view just over Anthony's shoulder. "Woah."

He had seen the Extreme Hills from the other angle—from high up in the mountains looking down at the blue pools of water and jagged rock below. But from down here, the rock spires seemed to stretch straight up to the clouds above.

Sophia stared too. Her teeth chattered as she treaded water, spinning to face Zack. "That was the best adventure."

"Best adventure ever," added Anthony.

Zack grinned. "Until the next one."

THE END